mountain born

Elizabeth Yates

Illustrated by Nora S. Unwin

journeyforth®

Greenville, South Carolina

Library of Congress Cataloging-in-Publication Data

Yates, Elizabeth, 1905—
    Mountain born / by Elizabeth Yates ; illustrations by Nora S. Unwin.
      p.   cm.
    Summary: A boy in a family of sheep farmers raises a black lamb to be
the leader of the flock
    ISBN 0-89084-748-7
    [1. Farm life—Fiction.   2. Sheep—Fiction.]   I. Unwin, Nora
Spicer, 1907-   ill. II. Title.
PZ7.Y213Mo   1993b
[Fic]—dc20
                               93-25967
                                    CIP
                                    AC

Mountain Born

Edited by Karen Daniels
Cover design by Jon Kopp
Line drawings by Nora S. Unwin

© 1943 Coward-McCann, Inc.
© 1993 by BJU Press
Greenville, South Carolina 29614
JourneyForth Books is a division of BJU Press

ISBN 978-0-89084-706-0

15   14   13   12

Contents

Books by Elizabeth Yates

American Haven
A Place for Peter
Carolina's Courage
Hue and Cry
Iceland Adventure
Mountain Born
Sarah Whitcher's Story
Someday You'll Write
Sound Friendships
Swiss Holiday
The Journeyman
The Next Fine Day
The Seventh One

1 The Black Lamb

It was a wild March day and the sky was full of tattered clouds, like a flock of heavy-wooled sheep. The wind was at their heels every moment and never once were they allowed to rest or change their course. On the far side of the mountains there was a pasture that the wind was heading them toward.

The wind was everywhere—banging doors in the house, flapping clothes on the line, whirling dried leaves into the air, searching out winter in all its hiding places, and preparing the way for spring. But not all the gustiness of the wind could rise louder than the baaings of sheep in the barn— sounds deep and tender, sounds high and imperative.

The woman in the house plunged her hands into the soapy water of the tub. It was a day for washing with such a wind for drying. Carrying out her next lot of clean clothes to the line, she set the basket down and ran her hands over the drying things, smiling at their crispness. She snapped out a man's shirt, blue and of a tough linen with strong seams, fastening it with pins to the line. Then she snapped

out a child's shirt, blue and of the same tough linen with the same strong seams. The wind puffed at the little shirt, filling it prankishly. For a moment it looked as if the little shirt were trying to be the big one, just by puffing itself up. The woman smiled again.

So like his father in everything, she thought to herself, then turned and went back to the house.

Soon it would be time to start dinner, for the men would be hungry after their work with the lambs. She went toward the stove. The door behind her slammed but she gave it no heed, thinking it was only another one of the wind's tricks. Then at the sound of a man's heavy footsteps on the floor, she looked around. It was Andrew, carrying something in his arms, something very small and wet.

Martha let out a quick sound and dropped the spoon into the soup she was stirring. She went toward her husband and held out her arms.

"It's the first we've lost today, one of twins; and the mother is busy with the other," he said slowly. "Thirty-four fine new lambs and now this little one—" he hesitated—"dead." He moved near the stove and laid it gently in the lambing box. "I'll tend to it presently; the hide is worth saving."

"Are there many more to come?" Martha asked.

"No, not more than three or four. Old Benj will be in soon for his dinner. I'll come later."

He was gone and the door had closed behind him.

Martha bent over the box and took the lamb into her arms. She felt stunned by the abrupt close of life on this day when life seemed to have such fresh beginnings—the bright sun, the charging winds, the lively sounds from the barn. Stroking the small creature with her fingers, she shook her head over it. Sometimes there was life in these lambs, a tiny spark that could be fanned into flame by tender care; but this one was dead. Andrew had said so. Such a fine lamb too, a black one. She laid it down again and went back to stirring the soup.

There was a shout of laughter outdoors and the patter of swift feet, then Peter stood in the doorway. His cheeks were tingling and his dark hair had been tousled by the wind. Early that morning he had gone with the calves to their pasture up the hillside so the barn might be free for the sheep.

"Mother, Mother," he began, fresh with all the joyous happenings he had to tell her; then his quick eyes caught the still form in the box by the stove. "Oh," his voice dropped to a whisper, "there is a lamb asleep! I must not wake it, must I?"

Softly he tiptoed across the kitchen and knelt down by the side of the box. His hand reached out and stroked the curly head.

Martha stood beside him. The boy looked up at her. "The lamb is asleep, isn't it?"

"The lamb—" Martha began, reaching vaguely for words; then she dropped to her knees beside the boy and put her arms around him, drawing him close to her. He had not seen death yet. "The lamb may be asleep. We will try to keep it warm. Now go and call Benj to his dinner."

Peter went running from the kitchen, and Martha bent down again over the stiffening form in the box. Perhaps there was still time to find the spark and coax it into flame.

She took a cloth and dipped it into the tub of clean hot water that stood beside her washtub; then she wrapped the lamb in it. She warmed a few drops of milk on the stove and put them in her palm, pressing her palm to the cold nose and trying to force a drop or two between the tiny, tight-clenched teeth. So soon a newborn lamb must have milk or there is no hope for it at all.

She heard the tramp of old Benj's feet and the high tones of Peter's voice telling of the lamb asleep by the stove. Good for you, Benj, she thought. He had worked with Andrew on the farm long before she had come to be mistress of the house, and he loved the boy. He could be trusted to say nothing that would distress Peter. Martha set the lamb down and hastily poured out two bowls of the thick soup, placing them on the table.

"Father will have his soup in the barn," Peter announced, "and may I take mine to have with him?"

"Yes, of course." Martha nodded, filling another bowl and watching the boy as he went slowly to the barn, carrying the two bowls carefully.

"Is there work for Peter too?" she asked, turning to Benj.

"There's work for all of us," the old man said. "It's something to keep near forty lambs feeding regularly, for some have sense and some have not, and some of the ewes are good mothers and some are not."

Martha bent over the box to change the cloth for a fresh hot one. Benj stood beside her, giving her help with his silent encouragement, adding words now and then that came from the slow deep wisdom he had gained through many years of shepherding. The lamb was still stiff and cold, save for the steamy warmth of the hot cloth against its fleece.

"Lifeless, is it?" Benj murmured.

Martha looked up at him. "Andrew said it was dead."

"Andrew does not know as much as God," Benj said. He knelt down and took the lamb in his arms. Pressing his bearded lips close to the black nostrils, he blew into them; then he slapped the ribs gently, first one side, then the other.

"Let us have a basin of water as hot as your hand can bear," he said.

Martha hastened to get it.

"And dry cloths, warm dry cloths," Benj went on as he immersed the lamb in the water. He dried it carefully, wrapping it in the cloths Martha brought until only its head showed when he laid it back in the box.

"Keep it warm. Give it milk as soon as it will drink, and then often." In easy gulps Benj downed his bowl of soup and went back to the barn.

Martha worked with the lamb all through the afternoon, keeping the cloths that wrapped its body hot, pressing drops of milk against unwilling lips. She was glad her menfolk were so occupied, for she did not want Andrew to chide her for her foolishness nor Peter to be troubled by it.

Sitting down in a low chair by the stove, she took the lamb up in her arms and held it close to her, remembering how she had felt when Peter was born and she had held him in her arms for the first time. Once the boy had come safely into the world, she realized how her prayers for him had changed. It was not for life and a strong body to hold its treasures she prayed, for he had these; he was a sturdy, shapely baby from the first. It was that he might be caring and useful in this world. Such a short way could she go with him on that path that was his life; only a few years she would have his hand in hers. For a few more years he would walk beside her; then he would be a man going his way alone, but if it were a way of kindness, the memory of that first day would always fill her with joy. Recalling it all, she clasped the lamb tightly and for that moment it was the baby

Peter, and her thoughts for the lamb were the thoughts she once had for her son.

Suddenly there was a convulsive movement in her arms and the lamb's tail quivered as if the wind were at it. Then it became as still and stiff again as it had been since Andrew laid it in the box. But hope had come to Martha's heart, definite and sure. Life was there. It was stirring in the tiny body.

She loosened the warm cloths that the limbs might have more freedom. She poured some milk into the palm of her hand and pressed it to the lamb's mouth. For a moment nothing happened. The next moment there was the faintest sucking sound—scarcely to be heard at all save by one whose ears were straining for it—and there the cupped palm was and no milk in it.

Martha sat back in her chair, half-singing, half-sobbing with the joy that ran through her. The little tail quivered again and the nose pushed greedily into the empty palm. Martha held the warm body to her, so close that she could feel the sound as it came from way within, the sound that found its way up the small throat and forced open the tight-clenched jaw, the sound of that first querulous ba-a-a.

Taking the cloth off, she set the lamb down on the floor. It wobbled on unsteady legs splayed wide, shook its head, looked up at her, and nuzzled against her skirt. Soon it sucked all the milk she would give it from a nursing bottle, and gradually strength came into the shaky legs.

Now twilight came sifting into the room, making pools of shadow. Martha had not thought to light the lamp, so busy was she with the lamb as they made their first acquaintance with each other; but coals glowed red in the stove and their light was a warm friendly one across the floor. The tramping of feet could be heard as the men came from the barn, and the clipped sound of Peter's boots as he ran beside them to keep up with their stride. Voices broke the stillness. The men were talking of food after the day's work, food to satisfy hunger and give them zest for more work.

The boy's voice rang out: "Perhaps Mother will have a stew for us tonight!"

Martha heard and smiled, catching the lamb in her arms as it ran in little jumps around the room. The door was flung open, and light from the lanterns the men were carrying streamed into the darkness.

"What's this?" Andrew exclaimed. "Martha, where are you?"

"Here, Andrew," she answered, and as her voice came to him, he threw the beam of his lantern in its direction. "I have no dinner ready, but look you what I have!"

Andrew stared. "The little dead ewe lamb!"

Old Benj nodded his head slowly and went across the kitchen to light the lamp on the table.

Peter clapped his hands. "It was asleep, Father, and I couldn't play with it before; now I can." His fingers stroked the lamb, and then, as if they were old friends, the two began playing together—the lamb with its awkward gamboling gait, the boy with his nimble limbs.

"But Martha, it was dead when I brought it in here," Andrew insisted, the wonder of what he saw making his face look like a child's.

"It needed warmth," Martha said gaily, so happy now that she could not remember the pain in her heart when he had first laid the lamb in the box by the stove.

"Something more than warmth she gave it," Benj murmured.

"It was Peter who did it," Martha said, as they watched the boy and the lamb at play. "But for hurting him I might have said as easily as you that the lamb was dead. Let it be his own pet, his cosset to bring up as he will."

"It shall be his cosset," Andrew agreed, "for the lamb still needs more care than its own mother can give it and had best bide with us here in the house for a while."

Martha smiled in delight.

"Such a fine little ewe lamb it is," Andrew went on, looking proudly at it, "and now we have not lost one of our young ones this year."

2 A Man's Work

The days following the lambing season were busy ones, for, as everyone knew, extra care taken then meant a fine flock later. The lambs were marked with notches in their ears so one year's crop, as well as one farmer's flock, could readily be distinguished from another. Ewes with their lambs were divided into small groups and kept in pens that they might be watched more closely and fed more evenly. The ewes were given good rich hay and grain so their milk would be abundant, and the lambs had only to turn to their mothers for the food they so urgently and constantly wanted, dropping down on their knees and reaching up to the heavy udders.

Mothers and children knew each other first by smell and later by voice. The plaintive sound of a bewildered lamb momentarily separated from its mother would soon bring the answering tone of a delighted sheep. Sometimes a lamb mistook another's mother for his own, his mistake being met by an unceremonious bunt; but once his nose and ears were bringing definite impressions to him, he knew one woolly mass as his alone.

"You shall have to mother the cosset until it can eat hay and grain with the others," Martha had said to Peter that first evening as she fixed a nursing bottle for him and half-filled it with warm cow's milk.

"How will she know to come to me for what she needs?"

"She'll know you by your voice," Andrew explained, showing Peter how he could teach the cosset to respond to a low whistle which he would use in calling her.

Peter imitated the whistle. "Like this?" he asked.

"Yes," Andrew said with a nod. "Soon the cosset will know that sound is meant for her black ears alone, and no other ears will even hear it."

Martha and Andrew watched the boy during that first week as he cared for the lamb with tenderness and the kind of skill that comes not from experience but from something far deeper. It needed milk at frequent intervals, and Peter

kept a bottle of milk near the stove always ready to hold up to the eager lips. The lamb rapidly gained strength and was soon able to be turned into one of the pens to romp and play with the other lambs. But whenever Peter appeared with his low whistling call, the cosset would leave its frolic and leap over to the boy, following him eagerly back to the house or about his round of duties.

As the days passed, the cosset was allowed to mingle more and more with the flock, but it never tried to get a ewe to own it, though more than one eyed the dark creature favorably. When it was hungry, or when evening came, it would seek out Peter: first for food, then for those caresses and games which it relished, and then for the pen of freshly spread straw which he kept in the shed for it. The lamb was the first thing Peter ever had to care for, and its needs made him conscious of what he could do for it.

The winds of March blew in the misty rains of April, and up and down the hillsides the grass was rustling with growth, but before the flock could be turned out to graze, the lambs' tails must be docked.

At breakfast one morning Andrew said he would need everyone's help out in the barnyard.

Martha's face fell, for she knew what work was at hand. Up to now, when the lambs' tails had been cut, Peter had been sent down to the village on some errand or pretext. When he had returned in the evening she had made light of the whole procedure, turning it into a story for him. She looked hard at her husband. Could he mean that now the boy was to help with this task?

Peter looked at his father. "What work is there to do today?"

"Today the lambs are just two weeks old and we must dock their tails." At the questioning look in his son's face, Andrew went on. "Lambs are born with long tails, Peter, but you must have known that something happens to them before they are many weeks old."

The boy nodded. "Ye-es," he said, "but I—I thought—"

"What did you think?" The man's tone was firm but kindly.

"I—I thought they fell off—or the wind took them. I didn't know you cut them."

The man rose from the table. "Benj and I shall be ready in a half-hour. Finish your porridge, Peter."

"Does it hurt them, Father?" the boy asked.

"Yes, it does, but only for a moment, and it is for their good. A tail is a useless thing. Without it a lamb grows to be a better sheep, cleaner, stronger, worth more in the market."

Peter turned to his mother when the door shut behind his father. "Must the cosset, too, lose her little black tail?"

"Yes, Peter, they all must go."

Peter picked up his spoon and started to eat his porridge, but it tasted only soggy and cold and not good at all.

Martha looked at her son. So this was the beginning of growing up. This was where the road they had been traveling together first parted.

"Go play with the cosset while I do the dishes." She smiled at him.

He returned the smile and slipped from his chair, running out to the shed where the cosset waited for him in her pen.

Martha did her work in silence. She heated the kettle of pine tar on the stove, then went out to the shed for the docking iron that always made a shudder run through her when she took it up.

"Come along, Peter," she said.

Peter put the cosset in her pen, then helped his mother carry the kettle of pine tar.

In the barnyard Andrew and Benj were busy separating the ewes from their lambs. Martha hung the kettle over the fire that burned in one corner and laid the iron in the embers. By the time the anxious ewes were in one pen and the gamboling lambs in another, the docking iron was hot. There was a stillness in the air and the scent of pine tar hung heavily about. From the house came a restless baaing. The cosset was not used to being alone.

Benj said, "Shall I bring a lamb?"

Andrew shook his head and nodded to the boy. "Fetch the cosset from the house."

Peter turned and ran back to the house, wondering what his father wanted the cosset for.

Martha looked at her husband. "Surely you won't do the cosset first? It will grieve the boy so."

Andrew nodded. "If the cosset is first, the other lambs will follow well," he said. "Does it seem a hard way? Wait and see; it will be the easier way for all."

"But the boy—" she began.

"The boy will be a man one day. Is it too early for him to begin to think as a man?"

Peter stood before his father, one arm around the cosset's neck. The lamb stood meekly, safe and happy because it was with Peter whom it loved. It pawed the ground with a tiny hoof, for a game would have been its joy; but because Peter remained still, it too was willing to be quiet.

"Peter," Andrew said gently, "the cosset's tail must come off first. If she behaves well, the others will too. Stand still and hold her very firmly."

"Is it going to hurt her?"

"Hardly at all, for it will happen so quickly."

The boy's lips parted in another question, then he closed them and dropped on his knees beside the lamb, holding its head and shoulders between his arms. Martha dipped the wooden paddle into the tar. Benj drew the docking iron from the embers and handed it to Andrew.

There was the acrid smell of burning wool and seared flesh, sudden and momentary; then the heavy smell of the tar as the bleeding stub was swabbed with it. The cosset gave a convulsive shudder and bent its body to leap, but the boy's arms were strong and held her.

"Now, let her go," Andrew said as he tossed into a box the limp, flat tail that had once signified so many moods.

The boy relaxed his hold. The cosset shook herself and sprang away in a series of quick leaps.

Crowding at the bars of the pen were the other lambs, eyeing the cosset, eager to follow her. One by one Benj led them out and the boy held them while the work was done;

one by one the lambs scampered off to play with the cosset, jumping now even higher than they had before, free from the weight and the clumsiness of their loose, bobbing tails.

It had taken most of the morning and the air had grown heavier and heavier with the ugly smell of burning wool, but now it was over and Martha had started back to the house. Old Benj was busy cleaning the docking iron. The lambs, returned to their mothers, were seeking from them the comfort of their milk.

Andrew turned to his son. ''You did a man's work this morning.''

Peter smiled proudly and slipped his hand into his father's. ''Shall we work together now, always?''

3 Alone with the Sheep

A few days later the flock set off for their first grazing, Peter walking beside old Benj with the cosset gamboling at their heels. Rollo, the sheep dog whose work was just beginning, trotted back and forth with an eager sense of responsibility, running from one side of the flock to the other, keeping the sheep from straying. Sometimes Benj would call him back with a sound both understood; sometimes, through a series of signals, he would direct the dog to the right or the left after a willful sheep. As he did so, Benj taught the boy the signals so that he too would have that common tongue of understanding with Rollo that meant protection for the sheep.

It was a gentle spring day; the lambing time of the year, the old man called it, for everything about them was little and full of gaiety. The leaves on the trees were like tiny coins, flashing in the sunlight. There were early blossoms and bright flowers looking up from the grass. Even the white clouds in the sky were small and frisky.

The cosset spied a pile of rocks ahead and leaped up to them, nimble legs finding their way. Peter followed, swiftly but not so easily, clambering over the rocks to the flat top-most one. He threw his arms around the lamb and hugged her, for the day was warm and the world was beautiful and they were friends.

"I love you, my little cosset; I love all the world," Peter cried aloud as the lamb bent her woolly head to touch his cheek.

Then they leaped down over the rocks to join the flock again.

When they reached the pasture, Benj looked around it with satisfaction. The grass was green and the brook that cut across it, drawn from the hills above, was fresh and sparkling. The ewes baaed with pleasure, for they remembered the grazing from another year. Dropping their heads, they began to crop the grass busily. A smile spread over Benj's face. How many springs he had seen the delight of the first grazing after the long winter in the barn; how many springs he had shared the same bliss with the flock.

"It's good pasture that makes strong wool," he said, "and we'll see the good of this green grass at shearing time."

"I'm hungry too, Benj, just like the sheep." Peter looked up at the shepherd hopefully.

They sat down on a stone and opened the luncheon Martha had packed for them—bread and cheese and milk and even a small bottle for the cosset. It was warm and lovely sitting there in the sunshine, watching the sheep, giving signals to Rollo, listening to the old wisdom that fell

so easily from Benj, who had herded sheep for more years than Peter could count.

"Benj, what shall I do when I am here alone with the sheep?"

"No different than what we are doing now."

"Shall I be afraid if they start to run?"

Benj shook his head. "Rollo will see that they don't."

"All the same, I think I might be just a little frightened," the boy said reluctantly.

"You have not feared for the cosset these weeks," Benj reminded him.

"No, but—" Peter began.

"Care for the flock then as you have cared for one, and all will be well."

By midafternoon they were leading the sheep back to the barnyard, for it was not yet time for them to be turned out day and night. Rollo did his work well while the old man and the young boy talked together.

"Sometimes you don't watch the sheep at all," Peter said; "sometimes I think you're not even seeing them."

Benj nodded. "That's true enough, but I have them always in my mind. That's the shepherd's life—to remember his sheep."

After a few days Peter took the flock out alone. Martha felt happy as she watched him go, knowing that Rollo could be depended on to do most of the herding. Andrew, at work in the field, waved to the boy as he went by.

"When the sun begins to drop in the west, start for home," he called.

"I shall," Peter called back, "but I hope that time won't come too soon."

What a fine day it was, Peter thought as he looked around him, and the bright world seemed made for him and the cosset. What games they would play together while Rollo watched the sheep.

After the morning chores were done, Benj sought out Andrew. He had an axe in his hands and some poles over his shoulder.

"I'm going out to mend fences," he informed Andrew bluntly.

"Don't you think there's other work more important for today?" Andrew asked. "The fences could wait until the sheep are put out with neither boy nor dog to care for them."

"I'm going today," old Benj repeated, and turning, he went over the path the flock had trod a few hours earlier.

Andrew shrugged his shoulders and went back to his work. Benj had been with him so long that when he took a notion to do something, there was nothing for it but to let him do it.

Peter, far up on the hillside, was full of glee. He and the cosset, quite alone for the first time, were discovering new

games and ways of playing as the morning went on. Sometimes the other lambs joined them and they all played together.

Kings-on-the-mountain was the favorite game. Bunting, scrambling, leaping, each strove for the highest rock on the hillside, and the king was the one who got there first and held the height till another forced him from it. Even Peter found himself bunted out of place more than once and compelled to yield to succession. There was a game of chase-me, which the lambs knew best how to play; and tag, which Peter was good at; and there was a hide-and-find game. They played most of the morning while the ewes cropped the grass and Rollo lazed in the sun—one eye always on the sheep, the other on the lambs. His limber body with its dark silky hair lay stretched out on the grass, giving a sense of easy repose which his always anxious eyes belied.

Suddenly, as if at a signal, the lambs all rushed off to find their mothers. Some found them immediately. Others sniffed until satisfied that a slow-moving woolly mass belonged to them alone. Others in their urgency made mistakes and were rudely bunted away, for the ewes were particular about giving milk only to their own lambs. Sometimes it was the twins who had the hardest time, for the ewe would let neither suckle till both had arrived, knowing that the flow of milk must be an even one. Hunger had seized the lambs, drawing them to their mothers as if by invisible cords, there to drop on their knees and suck earnestly, for life itself came from the dark soft bag heavy with milk.

The ewes knew when the lambs had had enough and would push them away, directing their attention to the grass that they might begin to learn to eat it. The lambs shook their heads vigorously to clean their lips from milk so flies would not be drawn to them. Then, replete and happy, one by one they bent their legs under them and curled up on the grass. Bliss wrote itself across their faces as they lost themselves in sleep.

The cosset was nuzzling Peter's hand. Peter stroked it for patience, then sat down and unwrapped their luncheon—the bottle of milk which, encased in an old wool sock, had kept a little warm, and his own bread and cheese.

The sun was hot, the air was soft, and after they had eaten, sleep stole over Peter as lightly as the May breeze. The cosset snuggled up against him, its small bland face in the crook of an arm. Rollo flopped his tail as he looked over at the two, then quickly swung his gaze back to the sheep.

The whole flock was at rest now, the ewes chewing their cud and looking off into space, the lambs curled up in sleep—sometimes one to a ewe, sometimes two. They were resting, but Rollo would not until they were all safely folded that night; then he could stretch out by the warm fire in the house with the ease of work well done.

The sun passed its zenith and the tiny leaves cast their shade at the base of the trees. The sun moved slowly on its course while the shadows of the leaves reached eastward down the slope. A lamb baaed; a sheep stirred. One by one they rose and shook themselves and moved across the pasture to the stream. Snuffing the water in their fussy way, they touched their noses to it. The cool, clear stream was its own assurance. The sheep drank fastidiously, and the lambs baaed curiously at other lambs whose faces looked up at them from the water.

Rollo followed at their heels, nipping the legs of a ewe who was apt to stray, urging another to jump the stream and join the flock on the other side. But one ewe was puzzled and afraid, and while Rollo tended to her, the flock drifted over the hillside as aimlessly as down blowing from an open pod. Rollo was troubled and barked sharply, but no answering sound came to him with its low-pitched promise of help. Leave the one ewe and her twin lambs so frightened by the water he would not; and collect the others he could not.

Peter woke with a start, rubbing his eyes while he wondered where he was. He felt the warmth of the cosset against his right side and shoulder, and the warmth was good. The day was still bright about him, but the rock against which he leaned was bathed in sunshine no longer. A cool wash of shade spread from it across the nearby grass. He sat up quickly. The cosset blinked and stood shakily on stiff legs. Peter looked around him. There were no sheep anywhere. He was alone on the hillside.

''Rollo,'' he called, while fear seemed to catch the sound and hold it in his throat.

There was no glad answering bark, but as he listened for it, he could hear the far-off sound of sheep baaing.

Tears burned in his eyes as he realized what had happened. The very day he was put in charge, the sheep had scattered over the hillside, and only a shepherd knew what harm they could come to. Peter trembled, not knowing what to do. A few days ago, working with his father, he had felt himself to be a man; now he felt small and weak and helpless. But he must not cry. No. No. He jabbed at his eyes to drive the tears away and started running down the slope.

He stopped short before he had gone far, unable to tell where the sheep were as the sound of their baaing came now from one side, now from another. Strange, dreadful thoughts pressed upon him as he thought of the sheep straying all over the hillside. Perhaps something had happened to Rollo, and without his help the sheep would be lost forever.

The cosset was nudging Peter, its little body meek and fearful as something of the boy's desolation became known to it. Peter knelt down and put his arms around the lamb, burying his hot eyes in the dark wool and wishing he could bury his troubled thoughts as easily. There was a small moment of assurance as he caressed the cosset, and Peter knew that if he could remember one of the signals for Rollo—the signal to come—he would have made a start to finding the sheep. He looked up and shaped his lips into the low sound. Then, before he could utter it, who should he see coming up the hillside with slow deliberate steps but old Benj, an axe in one hand and a bundle of poles over a shoulder.

Joy leaped into his heart. Before it gave rein to his feet, it loosed his lips. Now he could shape and give utterance to the low, clear call that carried on the wind and would summon Rollo. That done, Peter ran down the slope to throw himself against the old man.

"Oh, Benj, the sheep are strayed and Rollo's nowhere near," he began, lifting his face with its streaks of tears.

"There, there," Benj murmured, "never the harm is done that can't be undone. Easy take it; easy right it." He laid down his burdens and took the boy up in his arms. Then he gave the whistled call again to Rollo.

But Rollo had heard Peter's signal and was already racing to them. Peter, from his perch on Benj's shoulder, saw him coming. Now he felt brave again, and confident.

''Let me down, Benj; let me down so I can help Rollo.''

Benj set him down at his feet just as Rollo came up to them.

The dog looked at them for one brief moment, then doubled back on his course, going slowly and looking back every few moments to make sure he was being followed.

Around the hillside they went and across the brook at a place where the one sheep was still baaing hoarsely. Benj gave her a helping push that sent her over, then he lifted her two lambs across. Up the slope they went now and through a small woodland into another clearing where the sheep were grazing at will, up and down the rough pasture, a straggled, disorderly lot.

"Stand here, boy, with the cosset beside you, and let none of the sheep go past you. Once they become unruly they often get headstrong."

Peter stood still while Benj worked slowly up the slope to head the sheep off from going farther that way. Rollo worked down the slope. Responding to a series of signals, he edged right and left after the strays, bringing them back to the gathering flock. Between signals, he would lie with head down and ears alert, or stand as still as a clump of wild ferns. It was slow work, but gradually the flock formed itself into a unit again and grazed over the hillside, compact and contented, a gentle baaing replacing the more querulous sounds that had marked their dispersal.

Now Rollo moved them along so they went toward the stream, the ewes—even the fractious one who had caused the trouble—stepping daintily through it or leaping it lightly, their lambs following. Benj stopped for a moment and took a big kerchief from his pocket. Moistening it from the clear waters upstream, he washed the boy's face with gentle but clumsy hands.

"We'll have no telltale marks," he said, as he folded the kerchief away.

Peter felt happiness running like a warm flood through him. "Thank you, Benj," he said, squeezing the hard hand in both his small ones. With a spring to his feet, he leaped across the stream, the cosset following him.

Already the flock was moving down the hillside toward the home fold, slowly, contentedly, a great gray mass of willing obedience. Rollo paced at their heels, occasionally running to one side or another, more to head off a sheep's intention than an actual move.

"It doesn't take much to keep them together," Benj said quietly, "but once they get separated, it's a lot of work to bring them together again."

"I know that now," Peter answered.

4 Worthy of a Name

Now the sun shone for days on end. Blossoms rode on the fruit trees or lay scattered around the trunks. In the fields the corn was pushing through the ground, and in the garden the early seedlings were showing above the ground—the vegetables Andrew had planted and the flowers near the house that were Martha's. Such fine weather meant but one thing for the flock—that it was time for shearing. Andrew went into the village one evening and came back a few hours later with the good news that the shearer would be at hand to do their work the next morning.

The floor of the barn had been swept clean in preparation, and soon after daybreak the lambs were separated from the ewes and left grazing in the meadow while the ewes were brought to the barn. Some of the yearlings bleated anxiously, but the older sheep, as if remembering, stood patiently waiting for their moment.

Andrew and Benj would grasp a sheep by its legs and with a skillful motion turn it onto its back, holding it down; then with a quick running of shears over its body the shearer would clip off the fleece. More often than not it came all in one piece like a coat, heavy and greasy and worth its weight in the wool market. The fleece was tossed into a box built for the purpose, and it was Peter's job to tramp the fleeces down. The sheep, released of the heavy load it had been carrying all through the winter and spring, leaped to its feet and clattered quickly out of the barn and into the meadow. But oh! the strangeness of it all, for now the mothers were not very much larger than their lambs and had no dignity at all.

The lambs seemed to eye them suspiciously, not at all certain they wished to claim these pink-fleshed, ungainly creatures as their mothers. Crowding together in a corner, they baaed arrogantly. The ewes crowded together in an opposite corner, baaing beseechingly. One by one the lambs, drawn by that insatiable urge of hunger, came forward and sniffed around until each one found the right one, then dropping down, drew milk for its needs. Scampering away, they shook their heads in delight, for the milk was the same though the source it came from was so altered.

The shearer mopped his head and cleaned his shears while Andrew tied the fleeces into bales and Benj swept the floor.

"They'll fetch a good price," the shearer said, "and wool is up this year."

Andrew smiled proudly. "It's good feed that makes fine wool."

"I wish all shepherds heeded that," the shearer nodded. "Some will let the sheep eat brush and scrub and then wonder why the wool doesn't weigh more."

"They'll eat the brush and scrub," Andrew agreed, "for there's no better way to keep land clean than with a flock of sheep, but they need rich pasture too, and hay in the winter and grain in the spring. They repay care more than double, as most growing things will.''

After the shearing, Andrew waited for a warm windless day for the dipping that would cleanse them. Nearly two weeks went by. The dip was strong and he wanted to be sure the occasional nicks and cuts made by the shears had all healed. A tank was filled with warm water and the dip mixed into it; then one at a time the sheep were immersed in it, even their heads, so no lice or ticks could be harbored anywhere while their fleeces grew again. The lambs were dipped too, and here again the cosset, going first, showed herself the born leader she was coming to be. This done, the flock was now ready to take its part in the summer that was at hand.

Up in the hills, a whole day's journey at sheep pace, were green safe pastures where ewes and lambs could be turned out for grazing. Benj and Peter set out one morning with the flock. It was a long journey, uphill all the way, but the sheep moved with a nimbleness their great coats had kept them from having, and some even thought they were lambs in moments of frolic.

It was afternoon when they reached the pasture—rounded, grassy nobs of hills with a brook racing down a slope and trees casting pools of shade. Benj had come up earlier in the spring with blocks of salt. He had strengthened the fences running at the base of the hill and made sure that the flock would be safe and happy.

''Aren't you saying good-bye to the cosset?'' Benj asked when it was time for them to go home.

"She's not staying up here, is she?" Peter replied in surprise.

"She's eating grass now like the others, isn't she? Then it is time for her to pasture with the others. She won't forget you."

Peter put his arms around the cosset.

Benj watched them, thinking that when next they saw each other Peter would still be a little boy while the lamb would be almost a full-grown sheep.

As they went down the hill, a small bleating followed them.

Peter looked back and waved so often that finally Benj said, "It's better not to look back. Keep your eyes ahead of you."

"But ahead there's only the path down to the valley."

"True," Benj said with a nod. "But there's much to see along it."

"I don't care for anything but my cosset," Peter said stubbornly.

The old man went on as if he had not heard. "There are many things in the world. If we care for them all a little, we won't feel the hurt too much when we part with one."

Peter often thought of those words as the summer went on, for the days were such busy ones. Indeed, he wondered if he and the cosset would ever have had time for any games. There was work in the garden; in the fields with the crops; in the woods gathering berries. Each day made its demands and—because the work had to be done and was to help them all—answering them seemed better than playing games.

There were quiet times too, when his mother told stories to him; and beautiful clean days like Sundays when they wore their best clothes and went to the village to church; and all through the summer with its hot sun and cool rain, the seeds they had planted grew and flourished till they became crops ready to be harvested.

One morning, after a day of rain, the sun coming over the mountains showed a fine dusting of snow on their peaks. That was the day they brought the flock down from the pastures. The sheep were hardly recognizable, so fat were they, with such heavy fleeces again, and the lambs—only old Benj could tell them from their mothers. In the midst of the flock stood a sheep, dark brown, and heavily wooled.

Peter gave his low whistling call.

The pointed ears pricked at the sound. The dark head shook. Then, pushing the others out of its way, the cosset ran toward the boy.

''See, Benj, she's not forgotten me,'' Peter said, hugging his pet.

''No living thing forgets a kindness, and you were kind to her when she most needed it.''

''She knows me, she knows me,'' Peter shouted; ''my little cosset knows me.''

''She'll know you all her life, but she's a cosset no longer. A grown sheep is worthy of a name.''

Peter thought for a moment. "She shall be called Biddy from this time on," he said.

With Rollo's help they counted the sheep as they passed through the narrow gate. Satisfied that all were there, they followed the flock down to the farm, for the lead ewes knew the way. They had traveled it often and could not forget. It was the road that led home.

Andrew and Benj spent the next day culling the flock. Peter, watching them at it, thought that it was like thinning vegetables in a garden so the remaining ones might grow stronger. The good ewes and most of the yearlings were turned into a meadow near the barn. The old ewes, those who were poor milkers and those who had not dropped strong lambs, and all ram lambs were kept in the barnyard. These were the ones that would go to market. They would fetch good money and the flock would be better for the culling.

"First the wool and then the mutton, that's the shepherd's life," Andrew said as he went over the sheep in the barnyard, "for people must be clothed and fed, and the sheep can do both for them."

In a day or two he would come back from the trip to the market town looking jovial for the money he knew was in the bank, bringing something to Martha which she had long needed for the house, the promise of a new plough in the spring to old Benj, and a book or a toy for Peter. He would have with him the finest ram in the countryside, and it would be turned out with the ewes in the meadow.

"It's the way the world goes round," Martha mused. "What one has meets another's need. We have sheep and the townspeople have money. We make a small exchange with them, and then we have money for the things we need."

"It's lonely with the ram lambs all gone away," Peter said.

"There'll be more lambs in the spring," Martha reminded him, "and when it comes time for shearing, Biddy's wool will make a coat for you."

That was how the year went, and now that Peter was older he could take a part in it. Other years he had been at play when the great activities took place—the lambing and shearing, the dipping and pasturing and culling. Now he could take a man's part and help his father, and because his father had another pair of hands, small though they were, he could afford to let the flock grow that much bigger.

The winter passed with its bright chill outdoors and warm cheer within. The sheep stayed in the barn when the snow lay deep and fed on the hay and grain that had been grown for them. On fair days the sheep went into the barn-yard, stepping daintily through the snow and pawing it away to uncover tufts of grass. But if there was ice the sheep were never let out of the barn. Andrew would take no risks with them, since they were growing heavy now with their lambs.

These winter days the farm demanded less time and the house could have more. There were hours spent in the big warm kitchen, Martha busy knitting, Benj mending harness or tools, Andrew reading aloud. Peter would sit on the floor hugging his knees, using Biddy for a backrest. Big as she was, the black sheep was allowed in the house as in her early days, and she still chose to sleep in her pen in the shed.

Martha called her a nuisance, clicking about the floors on her small sharp hooves, nosing into any salt she could find, nibbling at potatoes or turnips, or whatever took her fancy; but Martha forgave her anything. Always in her mind was the memory of the day when she had held a lifeless lamb in her arms and Benj had put his bearded lips to the small black nostrils and breathed into them. And with her mind's eye, Martha looked ahead to the shearing and beyond that to the cloth spun and woven from the fleece, a cloth so dark and rich in color that no dye could match or better it and that would outwear all other wool.

When the March winds blew first warm and soft, then chill and raw, the lambs came: such a wonderful crop of them, half rams and half ewes, all as white as the snow that still lay on summer pastureland, all so imperative in their demands. It was a busy time, and while Andrew and Benj helped those who needed help into the world and set them suckling, Peter took charge of the yearling ewes, who would not lamb until another spring. Biddy was the leader of this group and she did almost as much for them as Rollo did for the whole flock.

Winter did not yield easily that year but kept coming back for another twist. It was hard for the things growing in the garden, but it was good for the wool.

"There's nothing happens on a farm that isn't good somewhere," Andrew exclaimed. "Our crops may be backward, but look at the fleeces!" He was standing in the barn surveying the heavy piles that Benj and Peter were tying together.

In the orchard, under the late blossoms of the apple trees, the pink-skinned sheep gamboled as lightly as their lambs, among them a shorn and indignant black one. On the barn floor a dark fleece, weighing upwards of six pounds and with more than enough wool for a suit of clothes, lay by itself. It belonged to Peter and was his reward for a year's work. Soon the bundled fleeces would be on their way to the market town, but the fleece of the black sheep would not be with them.

There was a woman in the village who spun wool and wove it into cloth. It was to her that Peter went that May evening when the wind blew across the ploughed fields in warm drifts.

Near the cottage stood a gnarled old tree bright with blossoms, and the air was filled with the song of birds. Peter stopped to listen, not only to the song but to the whir and hush of the spindle that came from inside the cottage. At the door he raised his hand to knock, loath to break into the soft flow of sound but proud of the fleece on his back and eager to show it. The sound of his fingers on the wooden panel caused neither spindle nor bird to cease singing but brought to the door a little girl.

She smiled when she saw Peter, for she knew him as the son of the farmer who lived up in the hills. Peter nodded shyly to her, for he had seen her at church on a Sunday with her grandmother.

"What a fine fleece you have there," the girl said admiringly.

"It's from my cosset," he answered proudly, "and I'd like a coat to wear to school next winter."

"What's a coat for a sheep is a long way from being a coat for a boy," a voice said from within the room as the sound of the spinning ceased. "Come in, boy, and show me your wool."

Peter stepped into the room. For a moment there seemed to be nothing to it but its trade, for at one end was a great harness loom and at another was the big spinning wheel. A short distance from the wheel, slowly winding the spun wool, stood a tall woman with gray hair and a quiet face.

Peter shifted the wool from his shoulders and held it up to her. She fingered it knowingly.

"Black sheep's wool; that's good," she said, rubbing a bit through her fingers.

"I'd like enough for a coat and I want to pay you for it," Peter said.

She looked at the wool then looked at Peter. "Yes, and you'll want the back broad and the sleeves deep-hemmed, for your young limbs are stretching out so that it won't fit you long unless it's made that way."

"When may I have it and what shall I pay you for it?" Peter asked.

"Not so fast, young man, not so fast. You shall have it before the summer is over. But there is more wool by half than is needed for one coat."

"Then shall I pay you with the remaining wool?"

The woman nodded. "That is as good a way as any, and Mary shall have a frock from it—a warm brown one, for she, too, goes to school this year for the first time."

Mary clapped her hands delightedly. "With red buttons on it, Granny, please? As shiny red as cranberries in a bog?"

"Red is a good color and red the buttons shall be."

Peter walked home that evening with quick steps. He had made the first bargain of his life and, country man as he was, he felt that it was a good one.

5 Leader of the Flock

Peter lay on his back in the short, dry grass. The air was still with the stillness of late summer when the earth has ceased pushing growth forth and is sunning itself, awaiting harvest. Distant, but not far, the sound of small hooves could be heard as they went from one tuft of grass to another, and even the dull sounds of crunching and chewing came on the warm air. Good sounds they were, that meant all was well with the flock.

Peter looked up at the tree reaching skyward above him. From one of its low branches hung a dark brown coat—rough wool once, now worn smooth. The arms were wrinkled at the elbows. Something about them made Peter smile, for they looked so much shorter than his own arms. He rolled over in the grass to see what Benj was doing. The old man was sitting on a stone gazing into space. Whenever he was not minding the sheep or doing some ordinary thing like eating or sleeping, he would be doing just that. It used to puzzle Peter once, but it didn't now.

"Benj—"

The old man turned his head to look at the boy.

Peter nodded to his coat hanging on the limb above him. "I'm thinking I'll need a new coat soon."

"Shearing time is a long way off."

Peter sat up and, reaching for the coat, pulled it down; then he put it on to prove his point. The sleeves were an inch above his wrists; the front where the buttons went was frayed; there was a patch over one hip; across a shoulder a rent in the cloth had been neatly joined together.

"There's wear in it still," Benj said, wagging his head sagely, "and where there's wear in sheep's wool there's warmth. It's served you well for five years."

Five years—Peter sat on the rock beside Benj and looked off into space. But it wasn't space. Only those who had never kept sheep on a hillside could think that it was. It was memory filled with such good and lovely things that dwelling on them made them live again, almost as real and sometimes even more wonderful. It was the time ahead too, dreams of what the years might hold—all the good things which, if one cared enough about them, could be the only things.

Old Benj had once said, "A man must have a care to what he puts in his mind, for when he's alone on a hillside and draws it out, he'll want treasures to be his company, not regrets."

"Benj, can you remember when my coat was new?" Peter asked suddenly.

"Indeed so," Benj said, "and a proper man you looked when you wore it on your first day off to school—the sleeves longer than your arms, and the bottom of it a good length too." Benj smiled as he thought of the fine figure Peter had made.

"And the smell of it, Benj, do you remember the smell of it? As rich and greasy as if it were still on Biddy's back." Peter laughed. "Biddy was so surprised when she put her nose to it. She knew it was her wool."

"She did, indeed; there's not much that she doesn't know."

Peter thought back on those days—how the coat had kept the wind away from him and shed the rain when he walked back and forth to school, companioned by big thoughts as books opened up to him and words no longer looked like sheep tracks on a sandy road.

"And Benj, do you remember at the next shearing when Mary came to help? She had her woolen dress on and Biddy's lamb followed her all over, for she seemed more like her mother than Biddy with her fleece shorn."

Peter rocked with laughter at the memory, and old Benj smiled.

"That patch now," Benj reminded him, "I can see your mother putting it on."

Peter felt for the patch and ran his hand over it. The coat had been so new then, it had been hard to keep the sadness from his eyes at the big ugly tear until his father told him it was a badge of honor. ("All good clothes wear such or they aren't fit for much," his father had said.) Peter had felt better at that and could bear without regret the patch his mother had put on. He could even bear to have others in his coat, if they came honorably.

It was at the shearing that his coat had been torn. Peter was holding the forefeet of a sheep while his father grasped the hind legs. Somehow the shears had slipped from the shearer's hands, and the force he put into them sent them across the sheep's smooth belly, pointing toward her neck. Peter had seen them and, still keeping his hold on the slender bony forelegs, had thrown himself across the sheep. The shears caught in his coat, ripping it jaggedly.

"You won't be forgetting the tear on your shoulder, will you now?" Benj asked, his soft old eyes twinkling.

Peter laughed. What a time they had bringing the sheep down from pasture that year! Instead of being docile and obedient, they were possessed and willful. Rollo did his best to check them, but different groups had persisted in getting off the road from time to time. Peter dived under a fence to head off three sheep from a farmer's new-sown winter wheat. A piece of wire had caught in his coat, and in his impatient need for freedom he had fought it, ripping the coat and winning for it a doubtful badge of honor and for his mother an evening of work with her sewing box under the lamp.

That was a year they would not forget, for the sheep had been quite right in not wanting to leave their pastures. The valley people had misread the weather signs, and the sheep might have had all of another month of their high grazing.

Peter liked remembering these things as he looked at his coat, now so small and worn and battered looking. It was as if it held in its pocket all the joys and hard work and deep satisfactions of these five years that had gone by.

"If Biddy would only have a ewe lamb, a black ewe lamb just like herself," Peter exclaimed, for though Biddy had had three lambs, each one had been white, and each one had been a ram that had gone off to the market town after the summer grazing was well over.

"Biddy's a smart one," Benj said. "She'll have a ewe lamb all right one of these days."

Then they fell to talking about the time just a few months ago when Biddy had shown her smartness as never before; since then, old Benj would let no one speak of her except in a most respectful way.

It was shortly after the sheep had been taken up to the hills for their summer grazing, and on the farm it was one of the busiest times of the whole year with the planting and sowing that was going on. Andrew and Benj and Peter had been working in the fields since early morning and had just come back to the house and drawn up their chairs to one of Martha's ample meals. There was a slight commotion outside. Rollo barked, but it was his bark of greeting and no one thought a second time of it.

The men took up their spoons and began eating.

Martha said, "Dinner hour's a strange one for a caller, but whoever it is, there's plenty of food."

The outer door was pushed open, and before anyone could rise from the table, in walked Biddy. She stood for a moment staring at them with her amber eyes that often looked as if they saw far beyond what was immediately present.

Andrew was cross. "She found a hole in the fence. Now the whole flock will be down here and just the day when we've more work than we can do."

"I made the fences good and strong," Benj said, puzzled by Biddy's appearance, but more puzzled by her strange stillness—her lack of any show of affection, her lack of any interest in food.

"Something's wrong up in the hills," Martha remarked quietly.

Peter slipped from his chair and took a potato from the dish to offer Biddy. But her jaws were tight clenched. It was not food she had come after. Then Peter saw. He let out a sharp frightened cry. There where Biddy stood, a pool of blood was forming on the kitchen floor—dripping down her neck, matting in the thick wool, down a foreleg, onto the floor.

The others saw too and came and stood by the sheep. Benj felt with his hand all around her neck.

"Is it wire?" Andrew demanded quickly.

Benj shook his head. "Teeth."

The two men looked at each other. Wolves, or dogs gone wild, their eyes said, though no words left them.

"Get the gun, Benj. Come along, Peter, we may need you. Some food, Martha; one of us may have to stay up there all night."

Andrew had taken charge and was giving orders in the quick stern way that was always his in an emergency.

Biddy turned and went to the door. She had delivered her message. She would go back to her lamb.

Benj took down the gun which was handled on such rare occasions that it was filmed with dust. It had been years since it had been used to enforce death, as it would be now. Its main use had been to bring an easy end to the lengthy days of a faithful farm creature or to one suffering past any hope of recovery. Benj shouldered it silently. Peter took the hastily put together packet of bread and cheese from Martha, then they were off.

Biddy was well ahead of them on the road, but even were she not in sight they could have followed her easily for the little trail of red drops she left behind her.

"She's bleeding sorely," Andrew said. "We should have tried to stop it."

Benj shook his head. "She wouldn't have waited that long. She's got her mind set on her lamb."

Peter said nothing, but a quiver went through him. He was proud of Biddy—proud because she had been his cosset and was now the smartest sheep in the flock.

"The bleeding is lessening," Benj commented after a while; and then, when they had nearly reached the pasture, he saw with satisfaction that it had ceased altogether.

They never found how Biddy got through or over or around the miles of fencing that were meant to keep the pastures safe, but they found why. In a ravine, a clustered frightened group of sheep were gathered, still trembling as they had when they had raced for their lives across the open land. Their wild eyes could not see the three approaching them as friends but as something more to fear. At sight of Benj and Andrew and Peter an anguished sound came from the flock—high and plaintive from the mothers, sharp and questioning from the lambs. Near the entrance to the ravine were the mangled bodies of six sheep who had not been able to flee.

With long strides Benj moved in among the flock, talking to them, reaching out his hands on either side to comfort and allay. Biddy had joined the flock, her dark brown fleece instantly discernible among the tawny coats. Somewhere she had found her lamb and was whickering over it, proud and happy. Her quietness and Benj's slow tones spread assurance to the flock and gradually they became calm.

Peter stayed with the sheep while Andrew and Benj went off across the pastureland and over the rounded nobs of hills searching for traces of the invader. But they found none.

When dusk began to settle down, Andrew and Peter started home. Benj was left sitting on a stone, the gun across his knees, Biddy and her lamb beside him so the flock would not stray. Peter remembered him sitting there—as silent as a tree, as grim as a storm-laden east wind. He remembered, too, the long walk home. His father had been quiet, saddened

by the loss of the sheep. Peter felt sad too as he thought of the cruel and bitter things that happened in the world, things that didn't need to happen and that upset the orderly pattern of their days. He buttoned his coat tightly. The smell and the feel of it brought comfort to him.

"How was it that night when you stayed alone?" Peter asked Benj. He had heard the story a hundred times but he had never heard it enough.

"It was as still as most nights are, and there were as many stars in the sky or maybe a few more," Benj began, "and I sat on the stone and I sat. Now and then I'd feel the gun to see that it was all right, or I'd reach for Biddy to make sure she was still there."

"Didn't you get sleepy?"

"Maybe I did, but when need be, a man can sleep with his eyes open. Some of the stars went down and new ones rose. A wind came blowing over the hilltops, shaking out cold. The sheep stirred a bit, and then I knew—as sure as your eyes are on me now—that he was looking at me."

"What did you do?"

"No different than what I'd been doing for hours past, sat and waited. I figured patience could outlast greed any time. Just before the dawn, when you could have heard the dew forming it was so still, he came from behind the rocks. I let him get just so near the flock, the warm smell of them tickling his nostrils—then I let go. The noise sent the sheep scattering, but the bullet got him clean."

Peter shivered with the thrill of it. He remembered the next part of the story. How, when they were sitting at breakfast that morning, Benj had come in and nodded to them.

Andrew smiled, and it was good to see the hard lines driven from his face.

"Got him," Benj said.

"What was it?" Andrew asked.

"Wolf," Benj said.

He hung the gun up and went to wash his hands. A look of relief came over him. He hated the gun, but when he had to use it he could. He had no heart for killing, but if it was to save life, that was another matter. Benj sat down at the table and ate his breakfast, then went to his day's work as if he had not kept an all-night vigil.

Since that time the flock had been guarded. Peter and Benj had spent the whole summer up in the hills, and Andrew had hired another man to help him in the fields. They had made a camp for themselves and once a week Benj had gone down to the valley to fetch back supplies. Peter had felt safe with Rollo to help him when he was left for a long day alone with the sheep.

That was the way they talked during the long days up in the hills, remembering things, putting them together, listening and thinking and imagining.

"You must have read books and books to know so many stories," Peter would say admiringly.

"Books—" Benj echoed, and his soft eyes grew misty; "we had a Book in our home and my father read to us every night after the supper."

"A book?" Peter could not imagine a household with only one book. After all, even their little farmhouse had several, and there were houses down in the valley which had many books.

"Aye, a Book," Benj repeated, lovingly.

Then Peter knew what book it was.

"You mean the one we hear read from at church on Sundays?" he asked.

Benj nodded. "My father read from it every day."

"There are sheep in it, aren't there?" Peter asked.

"Sheep aplenty," Benj answered, "and a boy named David looking after some of them."

"David," Peter murmured. There was a boy in school named David. He felt as if he might almost know this other one. "How old was he?"

"Maybe about your age, twelve or a little older. He was a good-looking boy, ruddy-faced, and he knew how to play a little harp that he took with him when he was out on the hillside alone with the sheep. But it wasn't always quiet on the hillside."

"Wasn't it?"

Benj shook his head. "No, no more than it's always quiet here. One day a lion and a bear came along and took a lamb out of the flock. David went after them, and when he found the lion he struck him hard and took the lamb out of his mouth. The lion was angry and turned on David, so David caught him by his beard and put an end to him right there. He finished up the bear too and carried the lamb back to the flock."

"Was the lamb all right?"

Benj thought for a moment. "He was a bit frightened, for lambs have tender hearts you know, but David put him to his mother and the old ewe knew what to do to comfort him."

"What did David do then?"

"He sat down on the hillside and picked up his harp. It had only a few strings but they were enough, and as he played them he made some pretty words to go along with the sound."

"That's a fine story, Benj. Tell me more about David."

"I will, for there's a lot to tell, but we've work to do now."

They got up and went toward the flock, one on either side, as it was time for their daily gathering and counting. When they finished tending the sheep an hour later, they went back to their camp. Benj built up the fire and started to cook their evening meal. Peter was still thinking about David. Benj said he had lived a long time ago, but there was nothing very different between his life and theirs.

Peter said as much to Benj.

"Sheep haven't changed any all these years," the old man mused, "and their needs are still the same—green pasture, fresh water, and a little extra care at the lambing. They give man the same good things too: warm wool and a stout hide and sweet, tender meat."

Benj ladled something out of the pot onto Peter's plate, then he poured out a mug of fresh ewe's milk for the boy.

"Three things, I've heard tell, best support the world," he went on, "the slender stream of milk from a cow's udder into a pail, the slender blade of green corn from the ground, and the slender thread over the hand of a skilled woman.''

The words fell quietly on the evening and through them Peter saw his father milking in the warm barn, his father ploughing and planting and watching the seed sprout. Then he could almost hear the whir of the spindle as Mary's granny spun the rough sheep's wool into fine thread.

Biddy came near them, her white ram lamb beside her. With Peter between her and the fire, she tucked her legs under her and settled down. Peter nestled up against one side of her and the well-grown lamb was not far from the other side. Darkness came down and the fire made only a small glow in it. The day's end was near. Work was over; now rest was at hand for men and creatures.

Peter drew his blanket over him and looked at the stars coming out slowly in the sky. Here with the earth beneath him, and the heaven above, he felt like a tree with its roots in the soil and its branches reaching skyward—wind and rain, stars and sun his comrades, and a flock of sheep his care.

Benj, gazing into the fire, was talking softly to himself. ''The Lord is my shepherd; I shall not want. He maketh me to lie down in green pastures: he leadeth me beside the still waters.'' The words long loved fell from his lips as thoughts long harbored kindled anew within him. ''Surely goodness and mercy shall follow me all the days of my life: and I will dwell in the house of the Lord for ever.''

Quietly he got up and put more wood on the fire, then he made his rounds. The flock were all together, asleep or chewing their cud. As he went among them, they made small sounds of trust. They were safe. They had been safe all summer, yet Benj had a feeling that the hills were not safe. Often at night a low wailing sound that was wind or a wild one would come mutedly on the air; and often in the daytime tracks that were not those of a sheep would be found by some watering place. But there had been no trouble. None of the flock had been molested. Still, it was there all the same, that strange foreboding.

Coming back to the fire, Benj straightened Peter's blanket and tucked it around his legs. He stroked Biddy's head for a moment, and from deep within her came that low affectionate rumble rarely heard save when a ewe first stands over her lamb, but it was Biddy's special language for the humankind she loved.

Benj stretched out by the fire, then he looked up at the sky with its sprinkling of stars. He had one prayer, prayed as long as he could remember, and in it he asked no blessing or protection.

"Thank you, God," he said, and his voice was like Biddy's in its rumbling tenderness, "for another day."

To Benj, life was a journey heavenward, and each day was a step toward that whole of goodness which he knew now in part. He closed his eyes and sleep drew around him like a light curtain. A smile bent its bow across his lips. He loved his simple life, unchanging greatly from day to day or year to year, except as the flock grew and new lambs replaced the older sheep, a life that bound him to the creatures in his care and helped him to understand them.

6 Wolves

When the mountains wore caps of snow, Benj and Peter gathered the flock together to lead them down to the valley. The sheep stood patiently by the gate while they were being counted, Rollo at the rear of the flock and Biddy at their head ready to lead at a signal from Benj. Over a hundred sheep they were now, sleek and fat with the wool growing deep and firm. Peter felt sad at the loss of the six, but Benj shook his head.

"It was a cruel thing but we can't grieve over the past; that there were no more lost is what I think about."

"That was Biddy's doing."

"It was. She fought for her own freedom but she won because of her lamb. A sheep will do anything for its lamb; instinct, some call it."

"What do you call it, Benj?"

"Not by any name. It's just knowing that something's weaker and depends on the stronger and older for help." He looked at the boy for a moment. "You know how it is,

Peter; when anyone expects you to do something fine, you can.''

They let the sheep through the gate one by one, then closed it behind them. Biddy stepped aside and the flock moved slowly past her. Benj called to her to go forward, but with her lamb beside her she stepped back a pace or two nearer the gate.

"Biddy says our count is short," Benj made brief comment.

Peter laughed. "She can't count the way we can."

"Maybe she can't, but I'm not the one to go against her word. Hold them, Rollo.''

The dog, at Benj's command, sprang to the head of the flock and blocked the road so the sheep could go no farther along it. Benj and Peter moved among the flock counting again.

"What do you make it, lad?''

"Just two over a hundred.''

"That's what it is with me." Benj looked puzzled. "It's the six the wolf got she's missing, but how to tell her they aren't coming back with us is more than I know how to do.''

Peter thought fast. "Shall I take six of the flock and circle around the hill then come down through the pasture and join you as if we'd just found you?''

Biddy was pushing at the grass in an unconcerned way, her plump bob-tailed rump toward them, but Benj spoke in a low voice, for he would not have her hear them.

"I'd rather be fooled ten times myself than fool her once," he said, "but you'd best do it, Peter, or we'll not get home this evening."

Peter singled out three of the more tractable ewes who were immediately followed by their lambs. He started down the road, then swung off it on the side away from the place where Biddy was grazing. He knew of a gap in the fence where the wire had once been strengthened. Reaching it, he twisted back the new pieces of wire and made an opening for himself and the sheep to crawl through. They hesitated for a moment, bleating questioningly as they found themselves being led back to the pasture they had just left; but, at a few persuasive words from Peter, they followed him through the opening. They were used to being obedient and so long as Peter went first—whom they knew and who was so like one of them in his brown coat with its familiar smell—they went after him.

Peter looped the wire together behind them and started up the first of one of the low hills. It was a rocky place where the sheep seldom grazed. There was little enough to graze upon, but for some reason or other the sheep had never seemed to like that particular hillside. There were deep clefts in the rocks and Andrew had once told Peter that there must be caves under them. The sheep were hesitant. Peter called to them in the low, soft croon he had learned from Benj, a captivating sound, for once hearing it, they would follow anywhere. They took a few steps forward, then stood still again.

Peter knew that sheep disliked going over a hilltop, fearing the unknown other side, but the plan to fool Biddy would come to nothing if they didn't go over the hilltop and swing down from it to the gate.

"Come along," Peter said, stamping his foot impatiently, a thing Benj had told him he must never do.

The sheep stepped backward toward the fence, their hooves slipping on the sharp rocks. A ram lamb baaed arrogantly.

"You're just silly sheep," Peter retorted and, acting as if he didn't care what they did, started up the hillside.

There were boulders at the top and he picked his way carefully among them. Suddenly he stopped still, gripping a rock and flattening himself against it. Not ten paces from him was a gray wolf, and around her four well-grown cubs were playing—prettily, if anything that spelt such horror could be pretty. His hands felt like ice on the rock. Water coming from a spout would have had more strength to it than his legs had then.

A tuft of flowers, growing in a cleft in the rock beside him, was bending in the wind—bending away from the wolf family so heedless of their visitor. Peter was glad the wind was blowing against him. He inched himself back along the rock, through the tangled boulders, then turned and raced down the rough slope. There was no need now to call the sheep to follow him, for they had already taken themselves down to the fence and were standing there waiting. One lamb had even squeezed himself through and the ewe was standing with the wire between them, baaing plaintively.

"Silly sheep, indeed," Peter said to them. "You've got more sense than a boy who goes to school."

His fingers were trembling, but he undid the wire quickly and made an opening. The sheep crawled through first, following the one who was impatient to reach her lamb. Peter wriggled himself through. There was a rending sound, but he was in too much of a hurry to reach the other side to notice it. He raced across the grass, onto the road. Benj saw him and the six sheep coming from the opposite direction than he expected them.

"Benj—" Peter called, then he blurted out the whole story to the old shepherd.

Benj nodded. "So that's what we've been feeling all summer! So that's why the sheep never went to graze on that little hill!"

Peter shivered, so close the wolves had been to the sheep, so little any of them had known.

"The mate of the male I got last spring," Benj said, piecing things together, "and her litter."

"But why didn't they trouble the flock?"

"The cubs were too small and the female had her hands full caring for them, but let winter come and the cubs be full-grown, and every farm in the valley would know it." Benj had turned round and was looking back toward the hills.

"Wh—what are you going to do?"

"I'm not going to lose any time, that's one thing I'm going to do."

"You haven't your gun."

"I'm making a trap."

"But the bait?"

Benj had worked in among the flock as they were talking. He laid his hands on a lamb that had only half the growth the others had. It was a runty little ewe early marked for market as there was no bone in her worth breeding.

"If I can do it with the lamb alive, I will. If not—"

Peter knew what Benj meant even though his thought dangled like a cord in midair. To safeguard the farms in the valley, the flock in another summer, the cost of a single lamb would not be considered too much.

Peter stretched out his hand and stroked the head of the little lamb. It looked up at him and bleated softly.

"Take the flock home now, Peter," Benj was saying, "and tell your father when I come I'll have five pelts on me as well as my own—and a runt lamb beside me, I hope." Benj turned to Biddy. "Are you for leading them now?"

The ewe looked up. Her jaws moved sideways, then she baaed deeply and walked slowly toward the head of the line. Rollo sprang to his place. Peter waited until the flock had got on its way, then he took up his stride behind them. He turned once to wave to Benj and the little lamb.

Benj walked back up the hillside and it was David who walked with him. Not the stripling who strummed a harp but the warrior who spoke with authority, "I come to thee in the name of the Lord of Hosts, the God of the armies of Israel, whom thou hast defied." Only Benj did not say "armies," or if he did, he did not think it; he thought "flocks."

Toward evening, when the shadows were lengthening and the cows had gone out to pasture after the milking, Martha and Andrew were glad to see the flock winding slowly down the long road to the valley. Biddy, the dark one, was at their head. Behind her, the mass of tawny-coated sheep were pressed so close together in the narrow road that one might have walked on their backs. Rollo could not be seen, but a bark could be heard now and again coming sharp and clear on the still air.

Martha caught the first glimpse of her son in many weeks, and even at that distance she could see that he had grown taller. Her heart gave a leap of pride. He was trudging along a short distance behind the flock and the dust from their many hooves swirled up around him. Martha waved but he did not see her; then she hurried indoors to prepare the supper. It would be a feast tonight with the flock in the barn and Peter and Benj at the table again.

"Martha," Andrew called, "Benj isn't with them."

"Are you sure?"

"I've been watching for five minutes and there's just the boy." Andrew was not worried, only wondering.

An hour later Peter reached the home meadows. He folded the sheep in their enclosure, then ran toward the house with Rollo beside him. Biddy walked placidly about inspecting the place, her long-time right of liberty still assured her.

Peter was covered with dust. He was thirsty and tired; but the greetings came first—his mother's arms about him and the smile of his father standing nearby, pleased that the flock had come safely through another summer.

"Where's Benj?"

Peter told in a quick, excited way the story of the she-wolf and her cubs and of how Benj was lying in wait for them with no weapon but a half-grown lamb.

"Andrew, shouldn't you go up to help him?" Martha thought of the gun standing in readiness.

He shook his head. "Near midnight it would be when I could get there. No, Benj has his own plans and I'm not the one to interfere with them."

They turned and went into the house. Martha, assured about Benj, could turn her joy undiluted to Peter; but before she set the dinner on their plates, she took a bowl of freshly pared raw potatoes and turnips and, going to the door, called Biddy. With short steps the sheep came over the grass, baaing gladly. Martha set the bowl down and Biddy's nose was soon deep in it.

"Come in when you've a mind to, Biddy; I've left the door ajar."

There was a low, deep sound of happiness and then the sharp crunch as teeth broke into the crisp delight of garden vegetables after a summer of grass.

Peter was carrying a steaming dish to set on the table, and Martha was behind him with a loaf of fresh bread when she saw the tear in his coat. She stifled an exclamation until the dish was safely set on the table.

"Peter, another rent in your coat, and it must last you through the winter!"

He looked up at her in surprise, then his eye ran quickly over front and sleeves. "Where, Mother? I don't see any tear."

She put her hand on the place between his shoulder blades where the wire had ripped into the wool. Peter still looked puzzled, then he remembered what had happened when he had crawled through the fence.

After dinner—after Andrew and Peter had gone out to barn and pasture to see that the creatures were content, and Martha had set the clean dishes away on the shelves—they gathered together in the kitchen. There was a brave fire in the stove, and the glow of light and feel of warmth reached far across the room. It was good, for the first chill that prefaced the long cold of winter was already on the land. Peter sat on the floor and told his parents of the summer. Biddy, lying in a corner with her feet tucked under her, was silently chewing her cud. Every now and again, short deep baas came from between her lips, as if she would echo all that Peter was telling them.

Martha sat at the table under the lamp with Peter's coat in her hands. Slowly and skillfully she brought the two sides of the rent together, and all around it she wove back and forth with brown wool like that from which the coat was made.

"The flock look sound," Andrew was saying; "you've had no trouble with them, no sickness?"

"No, Father." Peter was proud of the summer behind them. "Not a single sheep took sick."

"No accidents?"

"One of the lambs broke its leg early in the summer, but it mended soon."

"So!" Andrew exclaimed. "What did you do to it?"

Peter had forgotten the horrid feeling he had felt inside him when Benj found the lamb and called him to help with it. It was bleating miserably, a part of one foreleg dangling like a pendulum. The ewe was standing over it, helpless and distraught. Telling of it, Peter remembered only the ease with which Benj succored the lamb and the rapidity with which it had recovered.

"Benj set the leg in place as neatly as you'd set a stone in a wall," Peter said lightly. "Then he laid two straight branches from a tree on either side of the leg and bound them all together with a piece of cloth he ripped from his shirt."

Andrew nodded. "The bones of the young ones are soft and knit quickly. How did you keep the lamb off its legs?"

"Benj carried it for near a week," Peter said with a smile. "He made a pretty picture with the ewe following him wherever he went."

Martha had been going over the coat carefully, catching a thread here, patching a frayed part there. She laid it on the table and looked at it, smoothing it with her hands.

"There now, you'll have the winter's wear from it if you treat it well. I'll wash it tomorrow and iron it out, then it will be ready for school."

School, Peter thought, and it was something to think about: boys and girls instead of sheep; books and pads instead of misty distances filled with thought.

By noon the next day Benj appeared, true to his word with five wolf pelts in a bundle over one shoulder, and over the other the hide of a half-grown lamb.

"I'm sorry about that, Andrew, but it had to be," he said. Then he told him the story of how he had tried to lure the wolves into his trap with the scent of the lamb only. "But it wouldn't do. It's meat they're after and only the promise of it could outdo the smartness of their brains. Once they had it, they walked neatly into my snare."

"If the little one has saved the flock, and other farms too, I'm not minding," said Andrew. "That's a fair hide she made."

Benj turned and went to the water to wash his knife. He spent a long time at it before he felt sure it was clean.

Wolves were not heard of again in that countryside. No tracks were seen in the snow during the winter; no hungry howling came on the frosty wind at night; and none of the farms knew loss.

"There are some things," Benj commented on it to Peter, "that can't seem to live right with the rest of the world. They cause trouble to the good things and so they have to leave. I don't like what has to be done at times like that, but—" he sighed heavily, "a man's got to be able to do it."

"David was able, wasn't he, Benj?"

Benj thought a long time. "He was so, and he wasn't afraid to stand up to a big one named Goliath who was causing trouble in his countryside. Easygoing is the way we all like best to be, but we can't let easiness take the fight out of us."

7 Biddy's Lamb

That was the spring that Biddy dropped a ewe lamb.

Martha was beside herself with excitement and could hardly wait until Peter got home from school to have him see her. She kept going to the kitchen window, watching to catch a glimpse of Peter coming up from the valley. When she finally saw him it was getting near dusk. He was never any earlier, but she was impatient for him and every moment seemed an hour.

There was a strong wind, squally with wet snow. Walking into the face of it, Peter had bent low and looked more like a gnome than a boy as he came up the long hill. He was hurrying too, for all it looked to his mother as if he were coming so slowly. At lambing time he could scarcely wait from one day to another to see the new lambs; to see what sheep had twins; to help if any needed special care.

He stood in the kitchen shaking off the wet snow, brushing the large soft flakes from his eyes.

''Biddy has her lamb!'' Martha said.

Snow or no snow, Peter opened his eyes wide, not even feeling the flake that fluttered off an eyelash and quickly dissolved in a pool of blue wonder.

"Is it—is it—" he couldn't shape the words, so eager was he.

"It is," Martha said, nodding and smiling, "a ewe lamb."

"Oh—" There was nothing Peter could say, he was so happy. After three ram lambs, Biddy had her ewe—one who could grow up beside her and stay on in the flock.

Andrew came in, shaking the snow off him. He had a lantern in his hand, for night was coming fast on the heels of the snowstorm. By the looks on two faces, he knew what news had been told. A smile brought its light to his, tired as he was from almost three days constantly in the barn.

"Come and see her, Peter."

Peter buttoned his coat and went out to the barn with his father, the light from the lantern moving between them as they walked.

In the barn there were other lanterns hanging from beams, and the place was full of soft light and warmth. The only sounds were the crinkle of straw and the tender whickering as ewes talked to their lambs. Benj was busy in a corner and paid no heed to them. Andrew walked easily, but with steps so light they could scarcely be heard or felt. Off against one wall a little pen had been made. Biddy stood there, placidly chewing some fresh hay.

"Come close, Peter," Andrew said.

He lifted the lantern so its light might fall not on Biddy but beside her. There, curled in the yellow straw, was a tiny black lamb.

Delight and pride and overwhelming bliss caught the words in Peter's throat. He breathed deep with joy, then he dropped on his knees in the straw and reached out his fingers to touch the tightly curled wool on the head of Biddy's lamb.

Biddy looked at him. A rumble of pride moved up her throat and found its way out in a long, low baa-a. Only one that she knew as well as she knew Peter would she let touch so young a lamb.

* * * * *

The year had hinges on which it hung, and every hinge had something to do with the sheep; but that was the life on Andrew's farm and the living for his family, and it was right that the sheep should mark it for them.

After the lambing, the next great event was the shearing; and, though the days went fast between, there was time for much to happen. With the one, snow was caught in the branches of trees; with the other, blossoms rode high above the earth. But even better to Peter was the fact that shearing came when the school in the valley shut its doors and the children were free to help their parents—some in the fields and houses, some with the flocks and herds. They were all working with the land in one way or another, and every pair of hands was that much more work done.

As Andrew's flock grew each year, the work with it increased. The shearer came for three days instead of one, and the barn with its well-swept floor looked as if the snow had drifted into it for the great piles of wool standing there.

Peter could work with the men now, and Mary came up from the valley to have an eye to the lambs and give a hand to tying up the bales. She had long since ceased wearing her brown wool dress with the cranberry red buttons, but Peter clung to his coat—short as it was in sleeves and body and frayed at the edges. When the day got hot, he would take it off and hang it on a peg in the barn. Sometimes he would press a tattered sleeve to his cheek, remembering the days when Biddy was his cosset and the years between when her coat had kept him warm.

Biddy sheared well, not struggling when the men grasped her forelegs and turned her on her back, for she recalled how it had happened other years and that no one meant her any harm. When the fleece came off, she sprang to her feet and trotted off to find her lamb. The fleece was tossed onto the scale as, being dark, it was weighed and bundled separately.

"Less than last year, isn't it?" the shearer commented, as the scales fell short of Biddy's usual mark.

"It is," Andrew agreed, "she's beginning to go off."

Peter heard them through the bundling he was doing. The cord he was tying slipped in his fingers and he had to begin the knot all over again. For suddenly he had realized that they were not talking about any sheep in the flock but about Biddy—his cosset, the flock's leader. Then the fear came on him again as it had in March when the black ewe lamb was a few days old and Andrew and Benj were looking her over.

"She's got bone all right," Benj had said, "and a fleece like her mother's."

"I knew Biddy would have a fine ewe lamb one year."

"It's well she's got it now, for she's getting on. Another spring or two and her lambs won't be worth culling."

Peter had heard them and everything around him had seemed to stand still. Other sheep got old, lost their usefulness for breeding and went to market in the autumn; but he had never thought of this as happening to Biddy. Somehow he had thought of her going on and on, year after year. But no, that wasn't the way things happened, no matter how much one wanted them to. All the farm creatures had their span of life and usefulness, and when that time was up the end was simple, something agreed upon long beforehand.

Hearing them speak thus of Biddy had hurt and bewildered Peter, and he had meant to talk to his father about it that evening; but in the meantime he had got over the hurt and reasoned out the bewilderment, so he had said nothing. Now they were at it again, telling each other that Biddy was getting on.

"She's just gone seven years," he put in stoutly.

"And she's just in her prime," Andrew answered.

"Can't—can't she stay there awhile?"

No one said anything. To the men Peter's question didn't seem to require an answer. Andrew turned toward the next sheep to be sheared. Benj looked out the barn door at the sun. It was at its meridian, and by that Benj knew they should stop work and turn toward the house for dinner.

"Nigh noon," he called out.

The shearer laid down his tools and the sheep was set free. He and Andrew started to the house as Martha opened the door to call them.

Benj turned to Peter. "Maybe it would be nice to have the sun stay overhead always; maybe it would," he wagged his head, "and maybe we wouldn't get anywhere if it did."

A smile broke over Peter's face—that would be an odd thing if the sun and he stayed where they both were. He'd never grow up and evening would never come on. Of course, things were like that. Everything had to go forward and everyone had to go along too, whether the way could be seen very far ahead and one like it or not.

Now Mary was coming toward him from the orchard, running—her hair flying on the wind and her bare feet swift through the long grass. She was as tall as he was and she had good sense about the sheep. The lambs turned to her as trustingly as they did to their mothers. Peter had once thought that was because Mary wore a dress made from spun and woven sheep's wool and they liked the smell of her, but he saw they did it whatever dress she wore. Mary came flashing through the barn door and stood beside him, panting.

Peter pointed to the brown wool, still lying on the scale. "That's a nice fleece Biddy gave this year."

"Indeed it is." Dropping on a knee beside it, Mary lost her hand in the thickness of it.

"Peter, it's so soft, softer than the other fleeces."

Peter smiled. "Two days ago, I took her down to the brook and washed her all over. I don't want her wool to be washed again. I want the nice rich Biddy-smell to stay with it after it's made into a coat."

"Why, Peter?"

"Because—" he hesitated. "It may be the last coat I'll have from Biddy's wool." He looked away from Mary and out the barn door to the sheep in the orchard. "Biddy's getting on, you know."

There, he had said it; hard as it was he had said it, and the words had not got caught in his throat and he felt better for having said them.

"Oh!" Mary exclaimed, not surprised, not troubled, just softly as if Peter had told her the sun was going down in a little while.

They turned and walked toward the house.

"I'm hungry, aren't you?" Peter asked.

She nodded. "Hungry as a sheep in a green meadow."

"Perhaps," Peter said eagerly, "perhaps Mother will have a stew."

They broke into a run, bare feet nimble on the grass.

Early that evening while the light was still clear in the sky and soft over the land, Peter and Mary walked down to the valley. The brown wool had been bundled into a tight pack, and Peter carried it on his back. The air was full of sound—the deep tones of the sheep and the gentle bleat of the lambs, reunited at last. For, after the shearing, they had been perplexed about their mothers, and Biddy's lamb had been one of the worst. Shorn skin and bony legs meant little of the familiar. But now with evening had come recognition, and the sound that hung on the air—carried by the warm wind—was a sound of perfect bliss.

"Biddy's lamb was such a naughty one today," Mary was saying. "Three times, Peter, she went under the fence and I had to bring her back, and once she was just about to try the lettuce plants coming up in your garden!"

"She's got spirit." Peter nodded with pleasure. "She'll make a leader just like Biddy one day."

"I shouldn't think naughtiness would mean that."

Exploration—courage—how could Peter explain that was what the black ewe lamb had showed and that was what counted for so much. Most of the flock would follow wherever a leader went but were fearful of going anywhere without a leader. It was important that every now and then the flock should produce a sheep with wit, as well as fleece and bone.

"Wait and see," Peter contented himself with saying. "She may lead us many a chase this year, but she'll lead the flock another year."

They walked along in a silence that was no silence, for it was the time of day when the birds had much to say to each other and to the world. As they drew nearer the cottage, the sound of the spinning wheel came out to meet them, drawing them toward it with its soft whirring croon. Peter thought, as he heard it, that if one could catch the sound of time going by—days and seasons into years—it might be like that of the wheel.

"Is it always with you, that sound?" he bent his head toward the cottage.

"Of course," Mary said with a smile. "It's our work, our living. Just as you have the bleating of the sheep around you."

"Oh," Peter said, reminded of the chorus of baas that marked the year.

"Only it isn't always the wheel," Mary went on; "that belongs to the summer when the shorn wool is being spun into yarn. In the winter it's the click-clack of the loom when the yarn is woven into cloth."

"Which do you like better?"

She turned the question on him. "Do you like the little bleat a lamb makes or the deep baa-a of a sheep?"

He saw why she had done it and a smile spread slowly across his face. "I like them both."

"Well then, so do I like both the sounds of our work."

They stood at the doorway of the cottage, and Mary's granny came to greet them. She saw the wool on Peter's shoulder, but even more than that she saw the coat on his back. It was not the rents and the frays that caught and held her eye, but her handiwork and how it had served him for these many years.

"Another coat you're wanting," was all she said, "and you've need of it."

Peter handed her his wool. "The best fleece in the flock—Biddy's."

She fingered it. "It's strong, and soft too." Then she put it to her nose, "But it's got a smell of sheep to it so that Biddy's lamb will be following you as well as her mother."

"Oh, but I want it that way," Peter said.

"It's your coat," she answered briefly, "and if this one does as well as the first one, it will carry you right up to manhood."

That seemed a long time off to Peter.

She was feeling the wool, fingering it for its fibre, running a bit between her palms so it came out a thread.

"You've not brought me so much as the time before," she said, "it will take almost all I have here to make a coat for you, big as you are now, and what's left over might just go to make a little vest."

Peter's eyes shone. A vest! Now, that was like a man to have a vest.

"If there's no wool left for you to take as a dress for Mary, how shall I pay you for it, Granny?"

She thought for a moment, then she spoke. "Near the summer's end, there'll be work to be done here. Give me three days' choring about, and that will be fair pay; at that time I'll have the coat ready for you to wear back."

Peter had not looked over toward Mary, but somehow he knew what she was thinking.

"I'm glad to do the work for you, but I'd like to pay you in wool too," he said firmly.

Granny looked at the wool again. "Did your sheep lamb this year?"

"She did," Peter answered quickly, "as fine a black lamb as you've ever seen, but no finer than her mother when she was my little cosset."

"Then, when the black lamb is sheared next spring, bring me some of the wool for Mary."

"Indeed I will, Granny." Laughter flashed into Peter's eyes. He turned to Mary and saw the pleasure she was sharing with him at the way the bargain had gone.

Darkness was settling over the valley, and Peter, his business done, had no longer any reason to stay. "Goodbye, Granny; I'll be down at summer's end to do your work and wear my coat back."

"Shall I come to help tomorrow?" Mary was asking.

"Oh, yes," Peter said quickly, "for the shearing's not half done and there's work for all of us."

Mary was glad. She liked the work with the sheep.

Peter started up the road, past the houses with lights in their windows that cast faint gleams upon the way, into the open land where his lights were the stars. There was one that hung low in the sky over his home, and he had used it more than once to guide him. When the road started to climb, he could see the dim outline of their house and the glow from the lamp on the kitchen table. Even without the light he would have found his way, for the sound of the sheep still talking to each other and to their lambs drew him on.

8 Promises Kept

Soon after the shearing came the dipping, and soon after that the flock went off to pasture up in the high hills. Although the wolf menace was over, Benj and Peter stayed with the flock a week to make sure that everything was all right. They tracked the hillsides and searched the coverts but found no traces that spelt harm, and the sheep were content. There was no anxious bunching together when night came on, and during the day no sudden running into a compact mass that seemed to be baaing with one voice when the wind shifted. Rollo felt easy about the pastures too, for he picked up no vexing scents as he had last year, losing them again at a pile of rocks or by the stream.

After a week Benj said, "They're as safe as if they were in the home pastures."

"Then we can go back and help my father with the crops."

"He'll be needing us." Benj nodded his head.

They gave a final round-up, for there were well over a hundred sheep now. Biddy's lamb was the last one accounted for. It had been playing with some others on a pile of rocks and was loath to leave the height. When Benj discovered it, the spicy thing bunted him with all its vigor and Benj nearly lost his balance. Biddy watched them, her jaws moving slowly and her slit-pupilled amber eyes seeing only what she had a mind to see. Benj understood and rubbed her head affectionately.

"You're seeing her take your place one day, aren't you, old lady?" he asked, reaching in his pocket for the bit of raw turnip he always had for her.

Biddy made a low, pleased sound. She was proud of her ewe lamb, taking far more interest in it than she had in any of her ram lambs.

Peter stepped toward the lamb and offered it a tidbit from deep in his pocket, but the lamb would have nothing to do with him. Tossing its head and flipping its small hooves, it ran in leaps across the pasture. Peter looked perplexed. Biddy had never acted that way.

Biddy started off after her lamb and the two headed for the far side of a nobby hill. Up the slope they trotted, the lamb in the lead; up to the crest and over, disappearing from sight.

"There's a lamb for you, not fearing but just going ahead," Benj said, pride in his voice.

Peter nodded. He knew well the traditional fear sheep felt for the crest of a hill, always waiting until one of their number would be brave enough to take the first step into the world they could not see so therefore must distrust.

"Biddy's bringing her up all right," Benj went on. "When she gets through we'll have another leader."

They were satisfied that the flock counted rightly though two had disappeared over a hill. With a call to Rollo, Benj and Peter shouldered their few belongings and started through the gate and down the road. The flock had already begun to scatter over the hillside, and when they looked back to them from a distance, the sheep on the green pastureland were like clouds in a blue sky.

Summer was a busy time for everyone. As the flock grew, the crops that would feed them during the winter had to grow too. There was work from the time the sun brought light until the time it dropped low in the west, and often before darkness settled over the valley Peter was glad for his bed and for sleep. Near the summer's end, when the harvests were more than half in and Peter could be spared more easily than at any other time, he went down to the valley for his three days' choring. It was warm weather and a good thing, for he went coatless, knowing he would come back wearing a new coat and vest.

The weather had been brooding for a week. Low gray clouds that seemed to have no particular significance but still did not lift or empty themselves hung over the land.

Benj cocked his eye skyward. "The weather's up to something, but what it is I'm not the one to say."

That was something when Benj could not predict the weather, for to him skies, clouds, and winds told open stories which he translated to Martha's amazement, Peter's delight, and Andrew's distinct benefit.

Martha, her eyes on the blue-shirted figure winding its way down to the valley, said, "I hope it won't rain."

Benj shook his head. "It won't rain before he gets there, and when he comes back he'll be wearing a sturdy coat." Benj turned back to his work. It wasn't often the weather had him puzzled, but it did this time.

Peter moved through his three days of choring with such a sense of eagerness that it was as if wings were on his feet, bearing him without effort from one task to another. Hanging on a hook beside the loom was a coat and vest that looked as much like something of his father's as anything he had ever seen; rich brown to the eye it was and firm to the touch, yet soft, with pockets and brown buttons. When Peter was alone in the room he would press his face to it and rub his nose against it, smiling for joy that it had lost none of its rich sheep smell and that it would soon be his.

He tried it on one night while Granny surveyed it with the eyes of a craftsman who could never look enough at the finished creation so long held in thought and now become visible. It fitted Peter well, as well as any coat built to last five years or more, for the sleeves were long and Peter had to turn them back so they would not get in his way, and there was girth to it for him to grow to.

"It will do you well enough," Granny said, "well enough until you come to manhood."

Peter laughed. Manhood seemed a far country to him; yet Granny spoke of it as if it were somewhere near.

"Then you must bring me natural sheep's wool and let me dye it blue," she told him. "Brown is right enough for a boy, but dark blue is the color for a man."

Toward late afternoon of Peter's third day the wind began to blow. That in itself meant little, but where it blew from meant much. Straight as an arrow it was coming out of the southeast, its tip sharp with cold.

"I've never known that wind to blow anyone any good," Granny muttered to herself, as she brought in some hanks of dyed yarn that were drying outside. "Peter," she called.

"Yes, Granny," he answered, his voice small as it came from behind an armful of wood he was carrying into the house.

"I'd rather see you get on your way now than wait until morning, and I mean now, while there's light in the sky."

Peter set down the wood, and the moment gave him time to think. He didn't want to go. He and Mary had planned games by the fire this last evening, and Granny was going to read to them later; but there was no choice for him if Granny wanted him to go home then.

"Very well, Granny. May I put my coat and vest on now?"

"Yes, Peter, you've done more than three days' work and have earned them." She went to pour a glass of milk and butter a slice of her new-baked bread so Peter might have something to go on his journey with.

Peter buttoned all the buttons of his vest, then he felt the warm embrace of his coat as his arms went into it. Now he knew he could not be cold no matter how the wind blew or the snow drifted next winter. He put his hands in his pockets, feeling the depth and strength of them, thinking of all they could hold.

"Oh, Granny, it's a lovely coat," he exclaimed, and each word was like a heartbeat, for he had worked to earn it and his own sheep had borne the wool.

"I'm pleased with it," Granny said.

Peter turned quickly to Mary. "Next spring you'll have your wool, and I shall give Biddy's lamb extra care this winter so her fleece will be fine and strong."

Mary smiled. "It will be school soon, Peter. I'll see you there."

Then she stood with her granny in the doorway, and the two of them waved to Peter as he started homeward.

Peter, traveling north, had the wind at his back and did not feel its menace, so warm he was in his coat and so filled with thoughts about it. The wind sent scurries of dust and dried leaves along the road before him. It seemed to be snuffing out daylight as it blew, for darkness came sweeping over the land long before evening. When Peter reached the farm, he was surprised to see Benj tightening the barn doors, and he called out to him.

Benj waved. "Bad weather coming," he said, and went on with his work.

Martha had seen Peter on the road with the wind pushing him from behind, and for a moment the southeast wind lost its foreboding as it brought her son more quickly to her. Now he stood in the kitchen beside her, almost as tall as she, almost a man.

"You've got a man's coat and vest," she said to him. To herself she said, "But you're still my little boy."

"Isn't it fine, Mother? See, how strong it is, and big for me to grow into!"

She turned him around and looked at the coat from every side, nodding proudly, then she drew him to her and pressed her face to it. Laughing, she held him off again at arm's length.

"The smell of it, Peter! Rollo won't know you from the sheep."

He was pleased. "That's the best part of it."

It was some time after supper when the storm broke. The wind had been whistling and whining so all evening that they had almost grown accustomed to it, and the fire was burning with such a warm glow that they were scarcely aware of the night's creeping cold; but when the storm loosed its fury, Andrew looked up from his reading with a start and Martha laid down her knitting. Had it been rain they would have gone on with what they were doing, but it was not rain.

Andrew glanced toward the window, then at Benj.

"Sleet," the old man muttered, and the sound of it against the glass was like the sound of arrows being shot by a wild archer.

Andrew echoed the word, "Sleet."

"I left the sheep door open," Benj said, "and the pasture bars down. Everything else is tight."

"Good," Andrew said.

Each of them knew that if Biddy had started the flock down before the storm broke, she had a good chance of reaching the safety of the home fold before the roads got too deep for traveling. If she were up in the hills with the flock—well, that was something they had best not think about, for it would do them no good. There was nothing they could do until daylight, so they soon went to bed.

Next morning, the first glance out the window valleyward made Andrew feel as if he must still be asleep and dreaming, for the world was white. It was a strange sight, with harvests in the fields still to be gathered and leaves still on the trees.

Martha stood beside him. ''Has great harm been done?''

''Perhaps not too great. If it runs off soon there'll be much we can salvage,'' Andrew said quietly, ''and we've had a good year up to this.''

He looked out the other window toward the barn. All around it the snow was muddy, trampled by dozens of small hooves, and from within came sounds that had their own meaning.

Benj was in the barn when Andrew reached there. He was smiling; but there were tears in his eyes that made their blue more faded than ever.

''Biddy's brought the flock down;'' he said, ''all but ten are here.''

Andrew smiled with relief, then Benj laid his hand on his arm. ''But she's badly off.''

He led Andrew over to a bed of straw where Biddy was lying, her feet tucked under her and her head hanging low; every now and again a spasm of coughing shook her body.

Benj held her head to ease her. ''She broke a path through the snow—all the way down from the hills—all the night long—wet feet, wet fleece—'' he stopped.

Andrew nodded. That was the worst that could happen to a sheep. Something about them couldn't stand it. The old saying slipped into his mind, and once there it was hard to dislodge: a sick sheep is a dead sheep. Back and forth it went like the pendulum of a clock. Sheep were such hardy creatures until something laid them low, and then somehow they seemed to have no resistance at all. But Biddy was not just a sheep. She was their leader. Peter's one-time cosset. The dead ewe lamb Martha had nursed into life.

"Biddy." Andrew knelt down beside her.

She looked up at him and tried to speak, but the effort ended in a fit of coughing.

"There's ten others up in the hills," Benj reminded him, "shall I go for them, or—"

Andrew got up quickly. "No, you stay with Biddy, you know best how to care for her. I'll take the boy and go for them."

Martha, with Peter helping, was putting breakfast on the table. They ate hastily as Andrew told Peter of the work before them. Peter was eager to get up to the hills after the missing sheep. Rising from the table, he took off his fine new coat and started to put on the little old one.

"No, no, Peter," Martha said, "you must keep warm and there's no longer any warmth in that coat you've outgrown."

"But we have work to do, Mother, and my new coat may come to harm."

"It'll not be harmed if the work is good. Slip it on, Peter, and button it well." She held it for him while he laid the old aside and put on the new.

"Good-bye, Mother." He threw his arms around her in a sudden impulse of affection, then he hurried out to the barn.

Benj was feeding Biddy some gruel. She looked up when she saw Peter, gave a small sound of joy, and tried to stagger to her feet.

Peter laid his hand on her head and dropped down in the straw beside her. He snuggled her head against the new coat, and Peter could feel the pleasure rumbling within her though it never came out in sound.

"Yes, Biddy, it's your coat and I'll wear it all the way to manhood. Thank you for it, Biddy."

But Biddy was trying to say something to him. Peter looked up suddenly.

"Her lamb, Benj; did she bring it down safely?"

Benj looked surprised. Somehow he hadn't thought of the lamb. Quickly he went out to the barnyard where the flock were drying off in the sun and eating the hay he had scattered for them. He scanned them carefully, but it was easy to see there was no half-grown black lamb among them.

"Her lamb is up in the hills," he said to Peter and something of awe was in his voice, for the natural instinct of a sheep to save its own lamb had been transferred by Biddy to saving as much of the flock as she could.

Peter bent low and pressed his lips to Biddy's ear. "I'll bring your lamb back to you, Biddy, my little cosset."

Andrew, talking with Benj, was waiting for Peter in the barnyard. Benj reached deep into a pocket and brought out some small bits of turnip which he slipped into one of Peter's pockets, smiling knowingly as he did so; then they were off.

The snow was melting fast under the high sun, but it was still deep and they found their best going in the track Biddy had made—a way opened by a single sheep and pressed down by more than a hundred following in single file. Andrew went first, then Peter, then Rollo, and because they were all hoping so hard, they found little need to speak or words to speak with.

They made better time than they ever had in the summer, chiefly because they had to, but it was noon when they reached the hills. Andrew dismissed all the southeast slopes.

"They would have sheltered from the wind long before the storm broke," he said. "We'll find them somewhere on the lee side of a hill."

He spoke with confidence. Now that the long journey had been made and they had found none of the missing ten dropped from exhaustion by the way, he felt certain of finding them all alive, sheltering somewhere. That dislike of wind shared by all animals was so often their protection.

They had been searching for an hour when they came to a place where a thin steam rose from the snow. Rollo started pawing vigorously at it. Andrew took his spade and dug quickly, carefully. He had soon made an opening to a hollow where several sheep were huddled, the warmth of their bodies melting a place twice their size. The sheep baaed eagerly, stamping at the mud beneath them and knocking their heads against the imprisoning snow walls. They were all right, but very hungry, and as Andrew drew them out, Peter worked to clear a place on the ground where they might find a few spears of grass to nibble before the long journey home.

Andrew counted them as he dug them out. "Nine," he said, then he lowered himself into the cavern to see if one had got trampled or suffocated.

"The black one isn't here," he commented briefly to Peter.

"Isn't she?" Peter asked, finding it hard to believe.

"We'll have to get these sheep home quickly," Andrew said.

"I'll find the lamb, Father, and come down with her later."

"Peter, it's useless now." Andrew shook his head. "What's one lamb when we've got the flock. Besides, she may weather the snow and bring herself back."

Peter was firm. "She's Biddy's lamb. I must bring her back."

Andrew looked hard at his son and saw him as a little boy no longer but as a young man whose ideas had to be reckoned with.

"Very well, then. Keep Rollo to help and promise me to leave in good time before dark."

"Yes, Father. I promise you that."

Andrew turned and, calling to the nine, started down the muddy track.

Peter signaled to Rollo and started floundering through the snow toward the outcroppings of rock where the lamb had so often played. The lamb had resisted human contact from the first, and Peter knew he had no approach to her that way, but the lamb had always stuck close to Biddy. If he could get near enough to let her have the smell of his coat, that might be all that was needed.

The rocks were slippery. Peter stumbled often. Rollo was going wearily with no sign of interest in anything he was doing. Peter was hungry, and his legs had a numbness to them. Hopelessness was knocking hard at him and re-sisting it made him weary; but he had promised Biddy her lamb; he had promised Mary a fleece; he had promised his father to return before dark.

He stumbled and fell, striking his head against a rock. When he struggled to rise it was hard to see what he was doing, for around him everything was going dark. He must hurry, he thought, and tried to pull himself up so at least he could keep one promise and that to his father; then he fell forward again. Rollo whimpered and laid himself across the outstretched body of the boy. With anxious eyes, the dog looked up at the sun that was still high in the sky.

A dark, bunchy form pushed itself through the snow. Something familiar was calling to it. Something that promised warmth and food. The dark form came upon the familiar thing lying in the snow. Nuzzling the rough, warm smell, pushing its nose around to find some milk, it discovered raw turnip which was soon crushed between small teeth. Happiness at last. Peace at last. Home. The bunchy form curled its legs under it and went to sleep, its nose pressed close to the smell.

Rollo moved his head near Peter's and licked the boy's face, licked until eyelashes fluttered open and lips parted in recognition. Peter lay still for a moment. The sun was hot on him, but he felt wet and cold. His new coat was sodden. Slowly it came back to him where he was and what he had been doing. Then he was conscious of a weight against one side. Raising his head carefully just enough to see, he filled his eyes with the joy of what he saw—Biddy's lamb curled up against him as she did with Biddy.

It was a long way home, but the lamb walked meekly behind Peter, and Rollo trotted ahead. The sun, after a full day's shining, had effaced most of the marks of the storm. In the fields where snow had lain were pools of water and bedraggled crops. The road was deep in mud and the going was difficult, but Peter sloshed through it, forgetful of the distance and his weariness for the happiness that dwelt in his heart. All his promises now would be kept: he was bringing Biddy her lamb; he was sure of Mary's fleece next spring; and he would be home before darkness fell, but only just.

Now and again, during the journey, he talked to the lamb. At the sound of his voice, the sturdy little creature turned its head up to him—not with the understanding Biddy had, but in a way all her own that was the beginning of understanding.

The sun had gone from the sky and the wind had an edge of coolness to it when the barn came into sight, but there was still daylight over the land. Peter went straight to the barn, leading the lamb to Biddy's pen.

"See, Biddy dear, your lamb is safe with you again."

But Biddy was lying very still in the straw and made no sound.

Peter looked at her for a long moment, then dropping on one knee in the straw he laid his hand on the old sheep's back and stroked her tenderly. Words were whispering within him, but so softly were they uttered that only Biddy could have heard them; there was no sound in the barn but stillness and only the movement of shadows as night came in the place of day.

Peter stood up.

The lamb inched backward and looked up at Peter, bleating gently, resting its dark quivering nose against the wool of Peter's coat. Peter laid his hand on the lamb, smiling at the black face and sharp, bright eyes.

"You're our leader now," he said.

Then he turned and went toward the house, the lamb following him.